LOVE & MONEY

Also by the authors

The Magical Child Within You

Hugs and Kisses

The Lover's Book

LOVE & MONEY

YOUR SECRET SOURCE OF WEALTH

Genny Wright Davis
and Bruce Lee Davis, Ph.D.

Illustrated by Genny Wright Davis

MACMILLAN PUBLISHING CO., INC. · New York

Macmillan Publishing Co., Inc.
866 Third Avenue, New York, N.Y. 10022
Collier Macmillan Canada, Ltd.

Library of Congress Cataloging in Publication Data
Davis, Genny Wright.
Love & money.
1. Love. 2. Money. 3. Success. I. Davis, Bruce, 1950- . II. Title. III. Title: Love and money.
BF575.L8D353 158 81-8451
ISBN 0-02-530010-5 AACR2

10 9 8 7 6 5 4 3 2 1

Printed in the United States of America

We would like to
dedicate this book
to our clients,
who have taught us
that the more
we give in life,
the more we have.

bank

There's lots of money
in this world,
much of it in drawers,
pockets, and hidden away
in secret bank accounts.
But with all the cash around
there are very few people
who truly feel wealthy.

Some people work eight,
sometimes eighteen,
hours every day
in order to make it.

Others work their muscles
to the bone to break even.

There are those
who went to school
and worked their way
right up the ladder
and are still climbing.

Some continue climbing
until they make a killing,
stepping on everyone's toes
in the process.

BANG
BANG
BANG

Or until they collapse
from a gigantic headache
and fall off!

While others
give their all
to the company,
only to feel unappreciated.

There are artists
and musicians
creating for themselves,
doing their best work,
still feeling unsuccessful
and unseen.

Some people dream
of making it
but don't truly
believe they can.

And there are those who give up and decide to go without it.

While a few are simply born into a big pile of it.

People are sitting behind desks, counters, steering wheels, or on street corners, all waiting for the right customer.

Some people have $10,000
stashed away and
are afraid of losing it.

Some have $100,000
and feel as if they have
just started.

100,000

Then, a few have over
$1,000,000 and could be
on a long overdue vacation
but are still working,
working for some more.

Penthouse
1,000,000
Ring

It seems,
no matter how much
or how little one has,
making money
without being happy leaves
something to be desired.

10

Trying so hard to have it,
you begin doing everything
but what you want to do,
being everything
but who you want to be.

Until, no matter how large
your bank account
or how full your pocket,
your heart registers
nothing at all:
empty!

EMPTY
full

You cannot help
but finally stop
and ask yourself,
"How do I make it?"

Perhaps the answer
is *not* rushing back
into the traffic,
worrying about moving up,
or struggling to find
something new.

Perhaps the answer
is *knowing*.

There is something
very wealthy inside you,
something you have
yet to discover.

Beyond your fears
of never making it,
there *is* a part of you
that already has.

Suddenly you remember
there is someone
special in your life
who deserves
more of your attention.

Finding how much you have
may lie in discovering
how much you have to give.

The smallest things
become grand things
to be appreciated.

You are the biggest item.
Your feelings, fantasies,
and dreams are waiting
to be valued.

It's time you trusted
in yourself, your own
creativity, and were
rewarded for it.

You deserve it!

Forgiving yourself
and others
keeps the riches coming.

Taking a few minutes
every day to give thanks
only increases the feeling.

Until you find your
worse competitors
have become friends;
the boss, a partner.

Without really knowing
how it all happened,
you feel wealthy!

FULL
99

You feel successful
because you *are* a success!

Whether you fall off
the corporate ladder,
or your thoughts
turn to gold
and you strike it rich,

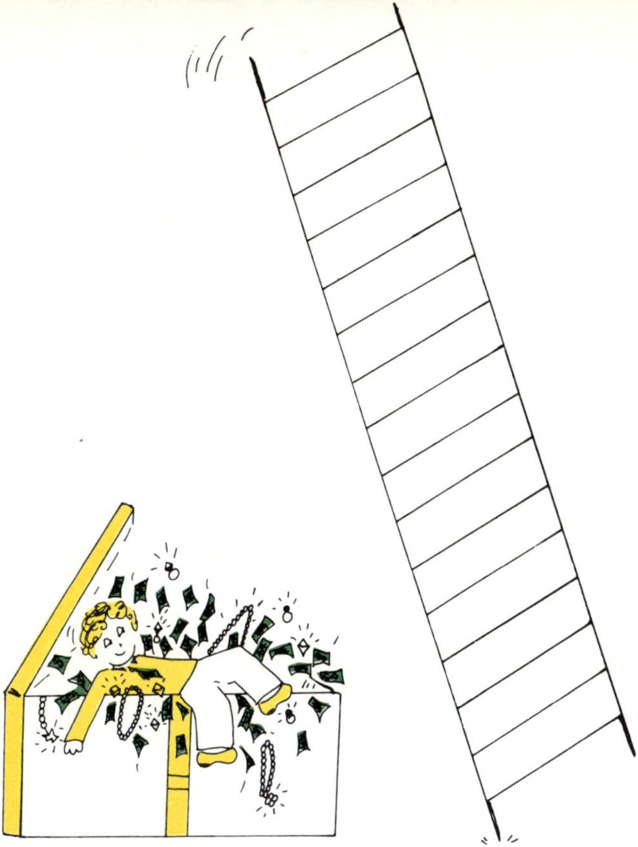

You have found the
secret source of it all:

Riches greater than
any paycheck,
investment,
or tax shelter—riches
that will always be yours.

Trusting in your heart
gives you all
that you ever need,

Because now
you have found
your true wealth
safely embraced
within you.